# Tell Me How You Really Feel

Claire Hopple

maudlinhouse.net
twitter.com/maudlinhouse

ISBN-13: 978-0-9994723-3-0

**Tell Me How You Really Feel**

# Table of Contents

**for Grandpa**

## Chapter 1

# Give Me Something I Can Use

Mallory would never say it out loud but she always thought the ramshackle barn on Cline Hollow and her ancient uncle would both outlive her. They seemed sturdy, toughened, relentlessly exposed but almost equally immune.

So when Uncle Errol announced he was having a funeral for himself while he was still alive, it made a kind of sense to her at the time. Why not have a funeral if you were going to live possibly forever? Or at least longer than everyone you knew. But that making sense was short-lived.

He didn't belong to a church per se, so being a former Harley man, he chose the one in town that hosted the Blessing of the Bikes every spring.

Morbidity seemed to envelop Mallory without her trying to conjure it. Her name, Mallory Clayton, was displayed on a sample plot outside the stonework place up the street, and she would pass her own tombstone on the way to the store. Eventually you become blind to your surroundings, and Mallory was no exception, even with something like this.

Uncle Errol began to plan with an earnestness that we hadn't seen since he discovered Craigslist. For upwards of 65 days, he procured, extracted, snuck, and quarried various materials he deemed useful for such an event. Poor Aunt Nancy didn't appear outwardly querulous. She was suspiciously helpful with planning.

Aunt Nancy never considered herself an optimist yet she always assumed the cobwebs she walked into were just that—cobwebs and not active webs—as she brushed them off.

Errol called up Mallory and told her to stop by when she could. Nancy was humming to herself as she ironed doilies in the alcove between the dining and living rooms when Mallory arrived.

"Would you do me a favor?" Errol asked. "Go down to the Ames and get me a pair of them nice black jeans."

"Unk, the Ames closed down in 1998."

"Hmm."

The subject was dropped after that.

They stared at some angel figurines on the hutch until he pulled a hardcover journal out from underneath a couch cushion.

"As you know, I'm settling my accounts, straightening up my affairs. This is my logbook."

He gave his best poring-over-figures-and-shifting-decimal-points look that could have been convincing in a different crowd. The logbook was blank and everyone in the room knew it.

"Of course, I've got your Aunt Nan to think about, but there may be something left in here for you, depending on how your speech turns out."

Nobody said anything for about a minute.

"You mean like…at the…service?"

"Yes, Mallory," he said, his voice becoming stern.

Mallory took a moment to reflect on the memories they shared but could only think of the day she came over to play with her out-of-state cousins. They played hard. When her mom came to pick her up, she could only find one shoe. They looked under furniture, behind doors, all over the house, out in the yard.

Mallory limped to the car that day. They never found the missing shoe. Even after two separate renovations. Her mother still kept the other one though.

Her aunt and uncle had a mailbox and then another post right beside it just for the newspaper. The newspaper holder was always empty, a mouth agape.

None of this was material she could use.

The funeral director smelled like Herbal Essences shampoo and still chewed bubblegum. Perhaps this was the only professional in the vicinity who would comply with such a memorial.

Mallory arrived early to help but ended up playing 20 Questions in the hallway with her first cousin once removed.

"Is it an animal, vegetable, or mineral?" she asked Cole tonelessly while eavesdropping on the adults.

"What time is it?" Mallory's mother asked.

"About 25 to 4," Aunt Nancy said.

Had anyone ever kept track of time that way, Mallory wondered. Maybe she was faking her enthusiasm after all.

With Errol's ego at stake, Mallory was slightly concerned this thing could turn out as unattended as a school bus in summertime. And yet here they all were.

"Yes, he's the one who used to cut your hair when you lived off Evans Road. Or no, he's the one who cut your lawn. He'll look familiar once we get in there," one stranger said to another stranger as they locked arms.

An intern from the local paper lurked in the narthex.

Meanwhile, Errol had mixed his own blend of benzodiazepines in order to lie realistically still in the open casket. The flower arrangements on either side of him were unapologetically ugly.

When it was Mallory's turn to speak, she began the only way she knew how.

"You don't really know a place until you've memorized its personal injury lawyers' catchphrases. And sweet Uncle Errol had memorized them all."

A few nodded from the pews.

"Some claimed he even had a photographic memory."

Mallory continued, lauding her uncle's character in ways that weren't overtly deceptive, and somehow made a whole speech of it, though who really knows what was said. She wondered what Errol thought of it, but he was unavailable for comment.

"Don't ask me who will replace him in this town, because I'm not sure it's possible," she concluded, stepping down and returning to her seat.

Aunt Nancy contributed next, but was simply relaying Errol's own parting words to his sworn enemy, who happened to be in attendance.

"I will be the puddle that forms on your driveway from your dripping AC window unit. In this way, I will show you that you can try to change the atmosphere but you can't control everything. You can't really control much of anything, in fact. I will then evaporate into the exact kind of humidity you are attempting to extricate."

Some people claim to have spotted a smirk on Errol's face from the casket, but this was disputed.

When he actually did pass away a few years later, he had already done everything there was to do. They were left with nothing. And nothing was a mighty gift.

His demise was a matter of time, as he was getting on in years and refused to go to the doctor. The doctor's office with its various containers of swabs might have been too much for him. Why are they always swabbing? What makes them think they can capture your insides on some cotton? Mallory could hear him saying things like this.

He probably could have outlived everyone but chose not to, she thought.

She moved to Ohio in order to regroup. She lived across from a rowdy set of neighbors who always left stray pieces of particle board entertainment centers on the sidewalk. It seemed like a new (yet incredibly old-looking) one appeared out there every few weeks. Sometimes in defiance she pointed the warped pieces in the direction of Pennsylvania as a mutant form of homage.

## CHAPTER 2

# Tell Me How You Really Feel

CALL ME BACK, the wall of the defaced bathroom stall said, which had to be important, or wanted to be important, Mallory wasn't sure. No phone number accompanied the demand. She was in a bar on East Carson. Uncle Errol was still alive.

The stall's message reminded Mallory of her cousin Joe's voicemail inviting her to a party tomorrow. The whole family got his exuberant invitations, coagulated with mumbles and sudden increases in volume. His voicemails mentioned a party. They always did.

She had just talked to Aunt Nancy about it earlier and still forgot in the between hours. Aunt Nancy said she was bringing yams. Aunt Nan was the only person Mallory knew who called sweet potatoes "yams."

Joe lived in one of the many places that passed for a suburb beyond the rivers and hills of the city. This was the suburb very much like the suburb fifteen minutes away that unfurled from the woods and clearings and bludgeoned auto body shops.

Somewhat disenchanted with his parties, due mostly to their frequency, Mallory admitted they had never been very effortless to navigate, even in their prime.

Joe wore Transitions lenses and kept his ringer at full volume.

When she arrived, he was pacing beside a card table covered with a plastic tablecloth.

"I can't feel my left arm. It's numb. That's not good," he said. "Oh, now it's back." He walked away.

When he returned, the room had started to populate with relatives and a few neighbors. His wine glass was filled to the very top and the corners of his mouth were marked with one tiny red triangle on each side.

"Tonight, I will be revealing everyone's secrets," he whispered to no one.

He watched over everyone's loitering, triumphant. Then, only about fifteen minutes later, he seemed eager for them all to leave.

Really, Joe wished not only to be suddenly rid of these people, but that the heavy curtains in front of his living room windows would hide a single person behind them. That someone would want to lurk in waiting for him. To be that desperate to ensnare him, even if for dubious pursuits.

Mallory ended up talking to her mom most of the time, who everyone else called Bootsie. A neighbor sidled up, warning them not to go out in the yard. Joe had just aerated it or treated it in some way, and it was fragile, the neighbor wasn't really sure. But she was sure he was getting exceedingly angry when people came close to approaching it.

A froth of surrogate embarrassment rose up in Mallory that she hadn't planned on dealing with.

"I hate..." she looked around the room, "...those table legs. They're too spindly."

She actually might have liked them, went back and forth about them, but just needed to complain.

She went to the bathroom, caressing one of the spurned table legs as she passed.

Oh yes, their grandmother was there too. She was smarter than all of them. This disappointed her initially since she wrongly assumed generations would progress. But she was so old that she just laughed at them now and wished them luck with the rest of their lives. At least she wouldn't have to see what might be the worst of it.

Grandma June didn't want to use the walker one of them had given her. It stayed at home in the closet. She was perfectly comfortable being old, had been waiting a long time to get to this point, so it wasn't about that. It just seemed to her like no one cared enough to update them. For years, all those old folks shuffling around with split tennis balls on the ends of their walkers. Like haven't they figured out how to do this right yet? But she let whoever think whatever they wanted to think.

Joe was slouched beside Grandma June on the couch. He picked up some wadded cocktail napkins from the coffee table and tossed them over his shoulder without looking.

"It's okay to throw trash behind your own couch. It's yours to do what you want with," he said, then scanned the room to see who had noticed.

In the bathroom, Mallory stared at the birthmark below her right eye. Birthmarks are really just the visible manifestation of being born with a human nature, she thought.

She wandered into Joe's office and unearthed a book called The Orient from the shelves.

As a constantly disoriented person, this seemed like a good place to learn about.

The author's last name was Sleeper, which made her think about all the last names formed from professions. Smith, Wheeler, Hunter. There were more. The bar could be set pleasantly low for someone with the last name of Sleeper.

She put the book down.

"You know what you're really doing. You're making your way out of here," she said aloud.

There was this event she could go to out near the Slopes, some performance art thing a friend had invited her to on Facebook. At the time, she didn't know this event wouldn't last long. That it would literally be a large man walking onstage with cymbals the size of Thanksgiving platters, holding them about a foot apart, waiting approximately thirty seconds in total silence, then walking offstage. The cymbals were maybe supposed to be symbols, she would think later.

"A Megabus driver is greater than a regular bus driver. It's simple math," Uncle Errol explained to a stranger in the hallway as Mallory slinked through.

The dog whimper of the door hinge and it was done.

She left feeling corn-shucked and echoey inside as kids turned cartwheels of destruction in the yard behind her.

CHAPTER 3

# There's Nothing Wrong

THE IMPORTANT THING was to not look like you were in disguise in the first place. Just go about your business.

Mallory's mom, Bootsie, had cloaked herself in men's polyester pants and a faded, plaid button-down she'd found at a garage sale. She'd packed two turkey and cheese sandwiches in waxed paper along with a Nutrageous. The chocolate was already melting. It was clear she was an amateur.

Nothing was happening. Not even a dog walker had passed on the street. Her inadequacy expanded. That was all she knew.

A green Jeep came down the street and just kept going.

On the way back, cars circled slowly at the roundabout, like preteens during a group skate at the rink.

"When I suspect someone's having an affair, what I typically do is go through their bank statements," her own mother said to her.

Bootsie'd been caught mid-investigation and confessed the limited number of facts and vague moods that had collected in the past few months.

"I doubt he'd even know the first thing about starting one of those," Bootsie admitted, "but something's definitely up."

By the end of Bootsie's confession June had already begun rifling through the kitchen junk drawer.

If he were capable of having an affair, he'd probably pick Dana, the neighbor on the other side of the ravine who blasted 90s country music and gave perms in her basement.

"No, I think it has to be something almost worse than that," she continued.

"Go ahead and stake out your own husband. Watch his every move. Make lurking your new hobby. Pretty soon you'll be a murderer. Then I'll have to visit you in jail. I'll die before you get out. Do you want to dismantle what's left of my life, too?" June said while gathering loose change from the drawer and putting it into her pocket.

Bootsie wanted to ask her mother if she'd even been listening when she noticed the hearing aids laid out on the counter.

"If you want to sneak around, at least try to be good at it."

She wasn't so sure about this sudden assistance. Her parents mostly ignored each other while she was growing up. Her mother still had wedding pictures hung all over the house but they were only bridal portraits. All different, but also strikingly similar poses, groom-less and teeming with a confidence bordering on smugness.

Bootsie couldn't help but think if the situation were reversed she'd be blotched with sympathy, unrelenting in her consolation.

"I can tell you want me to change the subject so I'll give you some news. Joe finally got a job. He's working at that new brewery. You know, the one that took over the old welding place. Errol was a welder over there for a few years so maybe it's some kind of tribute to his father. Who knows. At least he won't be hitting me up for cash."

Errol. Now there was a man who knew how to demonstrate retribution. When he thought Gary, his sworn enemy, was stealing from him, he went down to 380 Auction and bought a

"Watch Your Step" sign. He hot-glued it to Gary's front door, which had no step to watch for, so it read as a threat. Then a few days later he tried to do a citizen's arrest. When Gary slipped free, Errol told everyone Gary was a known fugitive.

June finally left. Bootsie crept up the stairs to read through her husband's notebook. In it were primarily lists of ideal fishing spots in the tri-county area. Unless this was code, she was at a loss.

Without conclusive evidence of any kind, Bootsie took to painting pottery at the store in the plaza across from Giant Eagle. Their mug collection had since doubled.

She also developed a habit of raising her eyebrows in the middle of a conversation because she knew the other person would automatically raise them too, without even noticing. It was a way to entertain herself. It was also a power, the most insignificant of mind controls.

Still, she sniffed the deer fur blanket while they watched movies and asked him overly specific questions about his day. One Saturday, she unearthed a box from the garage labeled Other. It contained a stack of comic books and a Tupperware full of baseball cards she'd asked him to get rid of when Mallory was a teenager.

Mallory was driving back home for a long weekend when a familiarity descended. She had dreamed this exact moment before, she was sure. What was dejavu called but with dreams?

She was kidding herself, maybe. Probably this was just a neural impulse to prevent cognitive dissonance. Her brain wanted to tell her that she'd made the right decision in moving to another state. That's what it was.

Mallory had just been turned down for a job that sounded like an incredibly cushy situation. Therapy dogs showed up to play on Mondays, Wednesdays, and Fridays. The company had its own cafeteria filled with organic, non-GMO foods. They would even pay for additional schooling if that's what she wanted. If she'd actually gotten the job.

About a month later she happened to catch the news story. Her would-be boss was accused of bombing the entire office complex. There were several victims.

She envied her mother, who didn't have to worry about these things. Mallory bet her mother wasn't burdened by thoughts like hers. Thoughts like how finding your own hair-shedding grotesque might really be thinly veiled self-loathing.

Bootsie begrudgingly took June's advice and finally looked through their bank statements. She really wasn't paranoid. He'd been keeping a major secret from her in the form of a withdrawal. Reese had bought a fishing cabin with a few of his buddies without so much as consulting her. She gave him a solid chewing-out about the matter.

So after all that, when they stretched out on the couch and he kept tapping her arm over and over, she didn't have to assume it was some kind of signal anymore. He would just tap and tap some more and she would know it was restlessness. The tapping had nothing to do with her.

## Chapter 4

# I'm Glad You Asked

Mallory's cousin, Joe, had just stepped out of his costume and was hanging it back up in the closet when he heard the front door open and shut.

Denise and Marco had arrived. Joe glanced at Denise's face to check if she looked happy to see him. Her face looked like she wanted to see him a regular amount.

"It's almost 3:00," he said.

"Yeah, we got held up," she said without further explanation.

She didn't even give him a chance to make her feel a little guilty about it. Joe always wanted a reason to stand there with his mouth agape like they do in television shows. He longed to feel that justified in someone else's wrongdoing, to really have one over on somebody, but the opportunity had yet to present itself.

He settled for a mumbled huff.

Denise wasn't having it. If he tried anything on her she would wear him down like the giant lozenge he was.

Marco, her hyperactive child, often disappeared in public places and had to be called back, Joe was learning. Strangers misunderstanding the situation would shout "Polo!" in response rather enthusiastically.

They'd met at work. She was the hostess and would say "Let's see..." to people waiting for a table, rubbing her pointer and middle fingers together as they hovered over the screen, just like a fly landing in the right spot and doing whatever it is they do with their front legs.

Two Joes worked there now: Joe C. and Joe M. This irked Joe C. to no end, especially since he'd been the one to get the other this job. Joe M. had called in a favor after close to a decade of lag time. This didn't seem fair to Joe C., but that was just how existence moved.

He started up the grill and they sat on the porch while Marco dug a hole in the corner of the yard, brooding about some mysterious childhood thing.

The day eventually turned out unremarkable and good.

Bootsie suggested Mallory stay with Grandma June instead of returning to her old bedroom for the weekend. June supposedly needed the company. Mallory could already picture her grandma looming like a pilot light in every room, readily dispensing her counsel.

June was actually at book club when she pulled up, so Mallory settled into the guest room in silence.

Black and white images taken at an old-timey photo place were framed on the nightstands. Resplendent in ruffled outfits, her family members posed with overly serious faces, mouths straightened more than natural like when people are lying. Their skin, forced into a bicolor realm, cast a lunar glow.

Mallory remembered seeing these here when she was young enough to think the timeline could add up. Were her aunt and uncle old enough to have lived through innumerable layers of skirts and tall hats, traveling to saloons, before the world of color? Entirely possible.

This was also around the time she'd pretend the floor was made of lava and the rugs and mats and carpets were islands.

She would partially melt sometimes but then quickly fuse back together. One afternoon she lost a leg and had to limp around for the rest of the day. Regardless, she would be pulled down by this capricious surface that was supposed to be a firm constant.

Grandma June and her friends were being shuttled across layers and layers of asphalt with perfectly adequate brick buried below all of it. Mallory greeted her as she was dropped off.

"Oh, that's great that you guys can take the bus together."

"That's not a bus. It's a car service. From the senior center," June corrected, then fully embraced her granddaughter until her perfume had permeated Mallory's skin enough to last until tomorrow.

Guests were strewn about the lawn.

Joe made it a point to talk to his cousin Mallory the most since she'd be leaving soon and returning who knows when.

"This is Marco. I am his father figure."

Joe tried to ruffle Marco's hair but it was buzzed and didn't noticeably move on impact.

Marco had a real father who was present in his life. He was a pear-shaped man who always wore a newsboy cap because someone complimented him on it once back in high school.

"Well, I gotta go set up," Joe said, leaving Marco with Mallory.

Marco picked up a Sam's Club-sized bottle of ketchup from the picnic table and squirted it in a line along the vinyl siding.

"That's an elegant mess," Mallory told him, adjusting from one foot to the other.

Denise fiddled with her recorder on the makeshift stage, then tested the microphones. She was dressed as a banana with cutouts for her face and legs complete with highlighter-yellow tights.

Soon, the other band members joined her, festooned in equally outrageous costumes. The rest of them held similar instruments, as in the kind you'd only see in an elementary school music class. A glockenspiel, castanets shaped like ducks, and wood blocks covered in sandpaper with convenient little knobs for handles. Together they made up a forest of gentle clomps and pings.

"This is oddly soothing," June disclosed to Bootsie.

June's hearing aids were beeping louder than the music.

On a break, Mallory asked two of the members what the band's name was.

"It's still technically up for debate," said a Troll doll named Amelia.

"We're called Lucky Plate," answered Zach, who appeared to be a nurse adorned in fishnet stockings and red heels.

"Unofficially," Amelia added, "until we come up with something better. Nobody knows what that means except you, Zach."

Mallory vaguely recalled her school cafeteria hosting Lucky Plate. The lunch ladies put a sticker underneath one tray on Fridays, offering a free dessert to the one fortunate enough to grab it from the stack. But she didn't want to bring it up and cause trouble. Plus, a tray is not really a plate, so the idea only made a certain amount of sense.

Instead of arguing, she ate a Bugle off the tip of her finger and brushed her hair with her other hand. The hand slid through her hair unimpeded by knots, which may have been the first time.

A guy needed to leave early but was having car trouble.

"Let me see what I can do," Joe said.

"Hon, you don't know anything about cars," said Denise.

"It's okay. It's in there. Solutions like these are all part of our collective unconscious."

Joe was only mildly confident but wanted to test the limits. He was still waiting for life to prove itself to him. Time was particularly suspicious. There was absolutely no way time was as mathematical and steady as it claimed to be.

"Nice costume, by the way," Mallory said to Denise.

"Oh, thanks. I was going to be Elton John until I heard about Joe's fear of glitter. I guess it's pretty serious."

"Huh."

A few people went over to help with the car and they seemed to get it running. Joe hooted in victory with dirt smudges on his face that might have been intentional.

"Break's over!" yelled Zach.

As Joe was heading toward the stage, he patted Mallory's arm.

"Yeah, you know Marco and I throw the ball around sometimes. It's good for him," he said, out of breath.

"Of course," Mallory smirked.

She kicked a tangle of Silly String off her sandal as they began the next song.

CHAPTER 5

# We're Way Past That

MALLORY THOUGHT THESE new conditions in Cincinnati were agreeable. There were a lot of murals in her neighborhood. A four-level bookstore was within walking distance. A man named Gypsy Frank photographed people on the street whose outfits he found fashionable.

That is, she thought these new conditions were agreeable until she caught herself talking to characters on a sitcom rather intimately. One character was being called out by another and she said, "That was so cold but so true," aloud. Then the thought-snowflake drifted down to gently force the realization that she didn't know this character at all and was actually thinking of someone she knew back home. A friend from school who accompanied her to the Hunan Kitchen once in order to fulfill an "ethnic food" requirement for Home Ec.

"We might as well visit the koi pond at the mall," this friend had said, grabbing a hunk of General Tso's with a hollow exuberance.

So maybe she needed to start socializing, she admitted to herself. The only striking interaction that'd occured since she got here was when a man at the bus stop had solicited her. She tried to retaliate by spitting on his shoe but it ended up being the dribbly kind that just hung from her chin.

Mallory decided to start small. She greeted fellow residents in the building. One of them, Kyle, cobbled together a living with several different jobs. He taught driving courses at local high schools and received undue double birds simply because of the "Student Driver" sign permanently displayed on the back of his Civic.

Mallory could say what she wanted to about Kyle, but he'd actually helped her land an interview with a flashy startup she had no business working for.

"It would be a personal comfort to me if you'd let me fix your car," Kyle said to her when they were getting their mail from the metal cubbies in the apartment entryway.

"Oh, well…"

Mallory had already said all manner of things to reject this offer but it was clear to her now that he wasn't really asking. He'd mentioned something last time about a steep discount if she publicly endorsed his rap career across all social media platforms.

"Well isn't this just typical," he said, pinching a box that was lodged so tightly in his mail cubby it seemed the cubby had been built around it.

"The postal worker can't be bothered to put mail in the right spots but somehow manages to fit this in here."

Impressed by the oddly specific skills and deficiencies of the USPS, Mallory used this particular marvel as an excuse to slip away upstairs.

According to the internet, one could prepare for a job interview by anticipating certain common questions.

After a meaty afternoon filled with a game called Strengths and Weaknesses, Mallory attempted to extricate some compelling challenges from her past that ultimately grew her as a person.

Only one memory stood out: She'd almost drowned in the Penn Hills wave pool as a teenager. Right after the lifeguards flicked whatever kind of switch turned on the sea simulacrum, there was so much commotion that the drowning itself had been drowned out. She was able to pull herself unceremoniously out of the water after several attempts, learning the hard way how to move with the waves and not against them. The lifeguards had looked on from their perches, completely unaware.

There had to be a better story.

If only they would ask her a softball question like what her favorite animal was. She could answer that. Anteaters are the perfect creature because they are where ugly and beautiful intersect to become one animal.

And then, there she was in an old house converted into a business with long hallways that abruptly ended, refusing to lead anywhere.

She was at an impasse, but just a literal one. Everything felt like it was in good metaphorical shape. At least for the time being.

Eventually, she stumbled upon what looked like a conference room littered with balloons, brightly colored plates and napkins, a mangled cake, a precinct of crumbs on the table, and disrupted chairs, completely abandoned to look somewhat ghastly, almost unrecognizable.

The woman interviewing Mallory found her wandering through the building and led her to a tidy, closet-sized room.

"So what brought you here?" she asked.

I'm fleeing Western Pennsylvania, Mallory wanted to say but did not want to say.

At some point, she was left alone to fill out a form even though she had already sent in a bunch of expository paperwork. When completing the address portion, she blanked. Her head seemed merely ornamental for several seconds.

Beginning to feel vertiginous with a mental claustrophobia, she remembered that in her last job she'd had to use sick days as mental health days. If she got this job, what if there weren't enough sick days? Just say you're going to the DMV, maybe. If you say you're going to the DMV people would just feel bad for you. They'd be too bored to ask followup questions. That excuse is just fake enough to seem real, she strategized to herself.

The woman, Paige, returned and walked her out. Paige wore heels that made pleasantly confident clacks down the hall. She smiled and muttered something indiscernible to Mallory, which Mallory actively chose to take as some profound aphorism.

Mallory returned the smile and said, "That…that is something truly unknowable, really. Completely unanswerable."

She walked to her car and hoped what she said was relevant to whatever Paige had actually said.

She noticed an old man in a coffee shop the next day who looked like Uncle Errol and took it as good luck. The old man matched her eye contact and held it, slowly closing the notebook in front of him at the same time.

## Chapter 6

# Neither Here Nor There

Nobody had a clue what happened to Joe's girlfriend Denise. She seemed to have gone missing. Joe felt like the last to know. Their steady communication stream had been compromised.

Acknowledgment always insists, but so does denial, and there was Joe in between.

Someone had stolen his bean bag chair and nothing else from his house a few days earlier, and that was a precursor, he saw now.

Denise might have slipped into the woods behind her apartment, or the woods behind her mom's, or the woods behind his very own house, even. Joe was overwhelmed with the possible wooded escapes into which she could've fled.

At best, she was on a clandestine vacation, sipping tea undetected at Marco's paternal grandparents' rental house up in Hidden Valley.

Perturbment puddled in his forehead at the thought. He knew this much: If he was going to bother to do an official manhunt, he'd better have something to show for it.

To cope with the disappearance, Joe's mom had vigorously sponge painted all her dining room walls in increasingly erratic patterns. You could tell where she feverishly began, where she grew impatient, and where she gave up caring altogether.

"Did you think about the last place you left her?" Nancy asked, picking paint off her thumb.

"I thought you were supposed to do that when you, like, lose a sock or something," Joe said.

"The concept still applies, more or less."

"Even with human beings?"

"Especially with human beings."

Joe didn't know what to say to that so he fondled a doily on the end table.

"Her pica was acting up again. She must've stopped taking her iron pills. I caught her chewing crayons one afternoon."

"Oh," said Nancy in a way that sounded like a revelation, but Joe knew she didn't really have anything to go on.

Denise had been gnawing on them in broad daylight. A symptom of anemia. She seemed to have a preference for Crayola's cerulean.

The last time Joe'd seen her was the day set aside for mentoring Marco. Joe knew the one-on-one time was good for him, even if Marco's father had already taken him to the Bahamas, the Alps, Toronto.

This was about the time Joe registered that life was molding itself into a shape of vague plausibility. Time was still not concrete but became an essence with slightly greater verisimilitude than before. He could admit that his perception was equally dubious and untrustworthy, but it was what he had to work with, the only thing he'd kept with him all these years, so he had an unquestionably fond, albeit biased, affection for it.

Zach had just texted that the band scored their first real show at the Slovak Club in Connellsville.

*We go on after the line dancing lesson clears out,* the message read.

Joe had decided to take Marco to Duff Park and do some solid reflecting on a bench. He'd barely consulted the list of conversation topics in his back pocket, things were going so smoothly.

They went to the mall next so Marco could be dropped off after Denise's shift at The Bon-Ton department store.

The escalator was broken and it irked Joe even though it had just turned into stairs and was therefore perfectly usable. It had simply changed into something that in most cases was your best option.

On the way down, Joe noticed some teenagers shouting and taking turns pushing at each other's collarbones.

This was exactly the kind of moment Joe had tried to manufacture earlier in the hypothetical. He rushed down the rest of the motionless escalator to break it up.

"Step aside," he said to the one with especially red cheeks.

They ignored him. A girl beside them was laughing.

"Go ahead and punch each other. I dare you," she said, laughing even harder.

It became clear to Joe that neither party was angry enough to do anything but posture.

They mumbled and made a few half-hearted, lewd gestures before heading in opposite directions.

Marco had sidled up to him at some point, just like Joe hoped he would.

"You see, in situations like these, you have to have a certain...*gumption.*"

Joe tried to formulate the rest of a speech but cleared his throat instead.

"If it's all the same to you I'd like to swing by Auntie Anne's and split a pretzel with you now," he finally said.

They eventually made it to The Bon-Ton entrance unscathed. The floor tiles were brilliant and perfectly spaced like nobody's teeth.

Bev was already hunched at the counter to replace Denise. Joe pivoted into Shoes. He wanted to avoid Bev at all costs. She was so neutral he thought she might completely dissolve in front of him one day. She was an antacid tablet of a person living in a ranch house at the true butt of a cul de sac.

Denise walked out of the door marked Employees Only shortly after that and they put a stamp on the day with dinner at Chuck E. Cheese's. That was it.

This recollection wasn't getting him any closer to figuring out where she was. She had left Marco behind, and he was staying at her mother's.

Joe would drive by Denise's mom's house every night just in case. He thought of it as a patrolling of sorts. She'd left her blow-up decorations in the yard. The deflated ghost and witch had their lives sucked out of them, making a completely different display but perhaps more effectively haunting than the intended one.

Inside the house, as you might imagine, Marco thought about his mother. He assumed she got fed up because she didn't have any hobbies. The frequent Marco Polo references made by strangers throughout his life and the irony of her going missing was not lost on him. He was convinced he was responsible for her dull, hobby-less life.

Marco knew it was impossible but had just finished reading *The Indian in the Cupboard,* so he snuck a peek in the kitchen cabinet to make sure she wasn't in there, then turned his attention to the science book on the table, skimming over the portion about surface tension.

## Chapter 7

# Few and Far Between

Joe presented the terrarium to Marco.

"Let's stick with one hermit crab for now and see how it goes," Joe told him.

Marco peered through the glass.

"Sometimes us living things have to be alone," Joe began, then shook his head.

Maybe he was going about this all wrong. This was supposed to distract Marco from his mother's fresh abandonment of him.

"The girl said it could live for 30 years, which I find hard to believe. You can be in charge of the daily mistings if you want. It might be fun to spray the little guy."

Joe had freed Marco from Denise's mother's house for the weekend. She insisted Joe buy a night light for the occasion and Joe pretended like he didn't already have one.

"Is it supposed to chirp like that?" Marco asked.

The pet store lady hadn't explained anything about what noises it should be making.

"Oh yeah, bud. That's what they do. That means they like you."

Marco was relieved to be here only because he had buried his secret treasure in Joe's backyard and figured this was as good of a chance as any to sneak out in the middle of the night and do some excavating.

The prospect of the wilderness dangled in front of Marco. This could be the first night of many he could live off the land. Maybe start his own rodeo, depending on where his journeys took him. He was that kind of boy, he knew.

You're really in it with someone when you get to see what kind of gas station snacks they choose. Mallory ran her fingers over the packages displayed on the shelves. They were unwavering in their lackluster nutritional value.

The charter bus had settled at this gas station on the way to a new hire orientation in Canton, Ohio.

A car alarm went off on the other side of the parking lot. Mallory was of the opinion that car alarms never alerted the right people. They wanted you to validate a violation that was most likely the void of one. They just wanted some attention.

She used to think the ticking of engines after cars were turned off was a secret language. Like cars were warning each other that humans were still in the area and that they had to wait to do whatever it is that cars do by themselves.

Passengers started climbing back on the bus. Two people scooted into seats directly behind Mallory.

"You have exceptional posture," one said to the other.

"Why would you say something like that to me?" the other snapped back.

Mallory had actually gotten a job offer from that flashy startup but had turned it down. She didn't like the idea of being indebted to Neighbor Kyle. So she took a job as an events coordinator at a nursing home instead. She liked knowing where life would eventually place her. This was preparation for an upcoming life stage, really. The nursing home sat directly across the street from a funeral home, and in this way, Mallory imagined the residents had the same thought. It was technically called an independent living facility, and Mallory had to keep correcting herself.

Kyle "had been carpetentering" (his words) as of late and was also trying his hand at limo driving. He was mostly keeping to himself for a change.

Mallory found her job refreshingly dull and this trip strangely soothing. There was an agenda, transportation, a hotel room all to herself. She was being told what to do and where to go at almost every minute of the day for the next three days and it was a kind of relief.

A woman sporting a visor, clipboard, and somehow even a whistle, herded the group off the bus and into the lobby. And with that structure in place, Mallory slept through the night.

Because why wouldn't there be Cheeto dust at the corners of his mouth on the most important day of his life?

Joe dropped Marco off at his grandmother's, threw on his jean jacket with the little round mirrors sewn on, and went to go find Denise.

He'd already checked with the brewery and the department store. Denise had officially requested days off at both of them. They refused to tell him how many days. He didn't know how to ask her freelance side jobs because he didn't really understand what they were.

Christopher Cross' voice came through the radio with—

*When you get caught between the moon and New York City*

—and Joe was absolutely losing it. This was their song. It was like 94.5 WWSW knew exactly what was happening.

He started singing along to himself but he was really performing for her. She could hear him trying to impress her and it was working through the power of his imagination.

The next song came on and he turned it down. The city and its rivers were coming into view. Right before Joe reached the tunnel he gestured across the downtown scene in his windshield and said, "All of this will be mine."

Then he let out a big chuckle and added, "Oh yeah, oh yeah. I wouldn't put it past me."

Just before Banksville Road, Joe reflected on the time his own father had kidnapped him. Errol had set the whole thing up to pin it on his sworn enemy, Gary, in order to sully Gary's reputation but things hadn't worked out like he planned. Joe did get to spend a couple of days at Grandma June's, missing school and watching *Saved by the Bell* and eating Golden Grahams though, and that part was alright.

Something in his gut was churning. Before he left town, he imagined finding Denise and the two of them running to the nearest courthouse or maybe even Vegas, but now that he was actually in his car, he felt ridiculous.

Joe took the next exit and steered into an abrupt U-ie.

Denise should find him in a completely neutral state. He should be monkish and unphased in his intactness.

Mallory heard what could only have been fake laughter coming from across the hall. These antics were oddly synchronous with the rattling of the ice machine.

Her phone screen was greasy with attempts at curing loneliness.

She got up and walked over to the wall shared with an adjoining suite. She tried to think of reasons but the reasons failed to present themselves. We never mean for things to work out this way, she thought.

Mallory inspected the door. Gripping the tiny metal knob, she slid the bar away from its latch. She unlocked the door between suites on the off-chance the person in the room beside her was, like her, searching.

## CHAPTER 8

# You Didn't Ask for This

"MY FAVORITE WORD is 'lagoon,' in case you were wondering. The sound of it. Saying it out loud turns you into a gently passing train. But there are rarely opportunities to use it in everyday speech, and that might as well be a crime."

Errol released the button on the recorder, took off the orange hunting vest Nancy made him wear once she heard he was headed to the woods, and tried to wedge the vest into his back pocket.

The miniscule cave was still visible from the creek. The old 2x4s remained in their places, forming a ramshackle bridge, though newly lustrous with creek scum.

This was after he had announced his premature funeral but before he went through with it, and before life was through with him.

He pressed the button again.

"But really, what I guess I'm saying is..." he trailed off as he lurched over a fallen limb.

He cleared his throat and started over.

"The thing about functioning is that functioning is not a constant. It will take any chance it gets to become mutinous, to run amok."

A squirrel was watching him nearby but pretending not to. This squirrel was not even looking at him directly.

"Can something just be amok? Or does it always have to run amok? One of language's many mysteries I probably don't have time to investigate."

After the funeral, Errol planned on taking a vow of silence and embarking on a pilgrimage to the last Blockbuster Video on the planet in Bend, Oregon.

"You know, Trish, after the service, people will be telling all kinds of stories about me and what may or may not have occurred between me and my sworn enemy. I don't have time to go through them all but I'll chronicle one for you right here. Sort of as a gift I'm bequeathing to you."

Errol nestled himself down in the leaves.

"It is true that I convinced the whole town to leave Gary hanging every time he initiated a high five. He eventually gave up and shot everyone the finger guns instead."

He sat until his joints ached and for whatever reason his body started shaking and sweating. He went back over the tape and heard a whalish wail that may or may not have emanated from his own throat.

He'd purchased the recorder to document his bouts of sleep-talk a few years earlier but quickly learned more than he was willing to know and stashed it in a drawer.

These new messages were only meant for Trish, his daughter who lived in another state but who had promised to make it to his service.

Joe would discover the tapes a few weeks later and they would confirm the favoritism he had suspected from the very beginning. His sister was better, that's all there was to it.

Trish was a former semi-professional mixed martial arts champion. Before moving away, marrying her husband, and birthing her son Cole, she lived in a treehouse on her parents' property for a full calendar year. She was dating a cobbler at the time named Dom whose shop was (and is) conveniently perched above Ferri's Fine Foods. Dom hired an assistant who never spoke to their customers, prowled around back corners holding men's oxfords in front of his face, and wore only corduroy in all seasons. When Trish wanted to break up with Dom, she decided to give him a series of bad haircuts instead. Not so bad that he could pinpoint the problem or even fix it. Just bad enough to notice and possibly associate the resultant feeling with her until things worked themselves out naturally.

Errol pulled into the driveway with a decommissioned cruiser. Nancy chose to respond by casually running her fingers along its faint lettering, still plain enough to make out "Sheriff" with a star below it. Errol appeared to be barnacled to the hood, huffing the remnants of a vaporous authority.

"Man, this was a steal. Don't I know it. Too good to pass up, Nan."

This seemed plausible enough. At least plausible enough under the circumstances. You see, Nancy knew what was really going on.

They'd been at Hoss' Steak and Sea House a few nights ago. By his third helping, Errol couldn't remember how to make his way back to their table. She eventually settled the bill and found him sober yet completely disoriented in the parking lot, staring at the deck hockey game nextdoor.

So yes, she went along with it. All of it.

And while she was going along with it, Joe was at his house practicing his speech for his father's service to a room full of stuffed animals, waving frantically and mouthing, "Thank you all for coming."

And Mallory was in her neighbor's front yard, formulating a response to this neighbor, who'd just asked for feedback on his baton twirling routine, and more specifically, how to incorporate his dog Waffles into the act.

And Denise in her kitchen, not really knowing any of them yet, only familiar with Joe from shifts at the brewery, making peanut butter sandwiches for Marco. Her pica demanded that she at least chew on the bread twist-tie while she spread the peanut butter. But she knew she was going to swallow the whole twist-tie before she got out of bed that morning. She knew she would make more sandwiches just so she could buy more bread and grant herself access to more twist-ties.

A pangea of foam broke apart in her coffee while she worked.

## Chapter 9

# Stop Me if You've Heard This

Gary wanted to say she was a former student of his. The waitress had a recognizable face but one that had unraveled a bit in his mind since retirement.

He fondled the generations of grease that had collected on the cylindrical salt shaker as he thought.

"...Nothing but flat fields of sleepy farmland up that way," June said as she limped through the door with Bootsie and Mallory.

They stood in front of a sign telling them that a hostess would seat them if they would just wait a moment.

"But you know I live in Ohio now, right, Gramma?"

"Yes, well."

"Tell us what's going on up there, since we're on the subject," Bootsie added.

Gary couldn't help but listen to their conversation. Look, the Eat'n Park was pretty quiet that morning.

Mallory proceeded to talk about someone named Kyle getting his first aid certification and wanting to practice on her. Something about puncture wounds being his weakest topic and asking her to lie down so he could go over cleaning, applying antibiotic ointment, and covering the wound. This Kyle guy sounded like a real creep to Gary.

"As I slid onto the cold tile, my loss of respect for myself was then sealed," she finished as they were led to a table in an adjacent corner.

The waitress returned to refill his mug.

Wanting a conversation of his own, he turned to her as she poured.

"Where did we land on Sea World? How are we supposed to feel about that place? You know, as…a society."

She couldn't take this in. Her free hand gripped the top of the booth and her pupils seemed to turn into mini-spirographs aswirl in their sockets.

She slapped down the check in response.

Gary rummaged in his pockets for change but was in no real hurry.

Seeing Errol's relatives still dismantled his ability to function. Everybody loved to talk about their spite for one another. What nobody ever talked about was the time Errol had gently caressed Gary's cheek in public out of what Gary liked to think was respect. It was at the Firemen's Carnival, under the questionable ferris wheel. Even the carnies had paused at the gesture, albeit briefly.

Sure, some guilt had cropped up from those years of cold war between them. Naturally. And so had some anger at his fake funeral and that stupid speech he made his wife give for him there. And maybe some flat-out rage due to the fact that he was actually deceased now. It's best to just forget about it. The whole thing'll blow over eventually.

Errol did have some negligible lead on him though, he had to admit. A few years back, Gary attempted to legally change his name to Errol Charles Clayton but later retracted the paperwork when he remembered that he'd already slandered Errol up and down the UFO forum he moderated on the internet. He would essentially have to kick himself out if he went through with it.

Leaning back against the vinyl, he could still hear the group's conversation well enough.

"He didn't tell you? They broke up."

"Last I heard she was MIA."

"Well, Joe thought she was. Denise had apparently been enrolled in some graphic design course for a couple weeks. She freelanced sometimes but never had any formal training so it was a big deal to be accepted. She swears she told Joe and everyone else about it before she left. Multiple times. Months in advance."

"Why didn't Denise's mom tell him what was going on?"

"I guess he never asked her. And Marco didn't really understand. She didn't want to tell the brewery or the department store she was involved in any kind of professional development unrelated to her work at those places so she just took some vacation days."

"Sounds about right to me. Not surprised by that at all," said what sounded like June.

"So I guess Denise called him up about a week in, saying they were keeping her pretty busy there, and he flipped out. She wondered why he hadn't called her if he was so concerned. Joe said something like he thought there was no use, that it was 'one of her displays.' And that's what did it," Mallory explained.

Things were getting too personal. Gary decided to reminisce about a dream he'd had the night before. He was being robbed. The robber constructed some kind of fort on his bedroom floor and began bundling up Gary's belongings. He'd shove items one by one into the fort, ignoring Gary's protests. When Gary zoomed in though, he saw that the robber was actually himself. Gary was stealing from Gary. He continued shouting at himself in the dream until his robber-self threatened to race him around the block.

"I'll allow it," he'd responded, and he woke up shortly after that.

The dream had been too much for him.

"Where do you see this going? What's your five year ham?" Bootsie asked her daughter.

"That's not how this works," Mallory said.

Gary wondered why Bootsie would ask about five year ham. But also what five year ham could be. Maybe there was a ham so large people could freeze it and eat off it for five years. Like wedding cake but more useful. What an investment.

Oh. Plan. Five year plan. He'd heard of those. It had taken him a minute but he got there.

He skimmed an article about glaciologists taking ice core samples to learn about us by discovering what's underneath us, then paid for his breakfast.

We know at some point that day he returned home and checked the mail but instead of mail there was a small tape recorder inside the mailbox. Trish had listened to the tapes her father had left her and made a decision. But Gary didn't know about all that. He didn't have the full story, and neither do we.

Chapter 1: "Give Me Something I Can Use" was originally published in *SOFT CARTEL.* (https://softcartel.com/2018/10/27/give-me-something-i-can-use-by-claire-hopple)

Chapter 2: "Tell Me How You Really Feel" was originally published in *Hobart.* (https://www.hobartpulp.com/web_features/tell-me-how-you-really-feel)

Chapter 5: "We're Way Past That" was originally published in *Reality Hands.* (http://realityhands.com/zine/were-way-past-that-claire-hopple)

## Acknowledgments

Thanks to my family (you know who you are). And to Murrysville, Pennsylvania, my hometown and the setting of this novella. Thanks to Nick Gregorio and Daniel DiFranco for priceless feedback at the manuscript stage. Mallory Smart and Bulent Mourad, you are both magical-unicorn-literary-champions. John Harlan Hopple, what can I even say to you?

CLAIRE HOPPLE IS the author of two story collections and one novella. Her fiction has appeared in *Hobart, Vol. 1 Brooklyn, New World Writing, Timber*, and others. She lives in Asheville, North Carolina. More at clairehopple.com

Lightning Source UK Ltd.
Milton Keynes UK
UKHW040814080321
379980UK00003B/839